James Otis

When Dewey came to Manila

Or, among the Filipinos

James Otis

When Dewey came to Manila
Or, among the Filipinos

ISBN/EAN: 9783743308961

Manufactured in Europe, USA, Canada, Australia, Japa

Cover: Foto ©Andreas Hilbeck / pixelio.de

Manufactured and distributed by brebook publishing software
(www.brebook.com)

James Otis

When Dewey came to Manila

WHEN DEWEY CAME TO MÁNILA;

OR, AMONG THE FILIPINOS.

WHEN DEWEY CAME TO MANILA

OR

AMONG THE FILIPINOS

BY

JAMES OTIS

AUTHOR OF "JENNY WREN'S BOARDING-HOUSE," "JERRY'S FAMILY"
"THE BOYS' REVOLT," "THE BOYS OF 1745," ETC.

Illustrated

BOSTON
DANA ESTES & COMPANY
1899

Colonial Press:
Electrotyped and Printed by C. H. Simonds & Co.
Boston. Mass., U. S. A.

CONTENTS.

LIST OF ILLUSTRATIONS.

WHEN DEWEY CAME TO MANILA;

OR, AMONG THE FILIPINOS.

.

CHAPTER I.

ON THE BANCAS.

PANDA, Raymond, and I had arranged for an excursion, on a fisherman's banca, from Manila to Cavité, and, without any very considerable coaxing, succeeded in getting our parents' permission for the pleasure trip.

So far as this permission is concerned, I speak only of Raymond and myself.

Panda was the son of our cook, a Filipino, although she looked more like a Chinese woman than a true native of the island.

Perhaps it would be better to explain first, before beginning the story of what happened to us at Cavité during the last of April and the first of May, in the year 1898, how Ray and I, two Yankee lads from Boston, chanced to be in the Philippines on that day when the fleet carrying the stars and stripes sailed past Corregidor, and destroyed the Spanish ships.

Ray and I are brothers; our father's name is Joseph Hyde, and he is the representative of a firm of Boston merchants who deal in hemp. With our mother, we two lads came to Manila one year ago, having travelled from Boston to San Francisco by railroad, and from there to the Philippines on steamers by the way of Hong Kong.

When Ray and I left home it was decided that we had as good a right to put into print an account of our visit to the islands discovered by Magellan, as any grown man who travels abroad for two or three months, and then sets himself down at home to write concerning what he saw.

We were very certain that every boy in Massachusetts, or any other State in the Union for that matter, would be pleased to know what two Yankee lads saw when they visited that archipelago, which, to our minds at least, was made up in equal parts of pirates and gold.

We had read wonderful stories of adventure met with in that group of islands which seemed to be situated almost in another world, and doubted not but that we would have full share in many startling happenings during the two years it was our father's purpose we should remain with him.

Therefore it was that both of us kept a journal of our travels, setting down everything we saw which was strange to us of Massachusetts, and believing that, when the time for our stay in Manila was come to an end, we should have written such a tale as would be in every way entertaining to lads of our own age, — Ray is fourteen and I am nearly sixteen.

To our idea the most important article in the "outfitting" was the mass of paper and dozens of pencils which we purchased for the purpose of writing the story, and nearly every day during that wearisome journey on the Pacific Express did we set down one or more items which appealed to us as being worthy a place in the wonderful tale we were to relate.

Then, once on board the steamer *China*, bound for Hong Kong, we filled the pages rapidly, for there was much of interest in the sea voyage.

At the Sandwich Islands we wrote no less than two chapters, and in Hong Kong it seemed to us as if we must bring the story to an end because there was so much to tell regarding the strange people and the odd things we saw.

After remaining ashore four days we embarked on the seven-hundred-mile voyage to Manila, and a disagreeable motion of the steamer, so different from what we had experienced while aboard the *China*, prevented us from continuing an account of our travels until after we entered the Boca Chica channel at the entrance to Manila Bay, steamed past Corregidor Island, and knew that we were within the limits of Luzon.

At the end of this long journey, during which we had travelled nearly half around the world, we were met by our father, whom we had not seen for three years, and twenty-four hours were spent with him before we began to look about Manila.

Here was to be the end of the story which we proposed

to send home to the Massachusetts lads, firmly believing
that by such means we should make ourselves well and
agreeably known to those whom we might never meet.

We described Manila Bay as it appeared to us on the
afternoon we entered ; told of the queer little custom-
house on the quay ; of the odd-looking oxen, the goats,
and the Span-
ish officers who
were to be seen
everywhere.

We walked
about old Man-
ila, as a portion
of the city is
called, looking at
the wall which
hems it in, and
set forth what I
considered very interesting descriptions of the peculiar
houses, the funny beds, and everything that met our gaze,
for nowhere in our progress did we see familiar objects.

To wear suits of white cotton cloth such as our father
ordered for us from the native tailor was in itself worthy,
as Ray said, a full page, and that building situated on the
banks of the Pasig River, which was to be our home while
we remained in the Philippines, needed many words to
describe it properly.

Fancy a stove for cooking which is only an earthen
jar, a dozen being necessary for the cook who counts on

preparing an ordinary meal, or windows in which are sea shells instead of glass; buildings that are no more than two stories high, built low because of possible earthquakes, and queer-looking Filipinos, — men who are more often seen with game-cocks under their arms than books; barbers who carry their chairs with them, and ply their trade on the streets.

It seems a cruel waste of labour and good material for a story, to throw aside all Ray and I had written regarding what we saw; but because of that which came to us when the American fleet entered the bay to give the Spaniards such a lesson as was needed, it is necessary, in order to make room for that which befell us when, with Panda, the Filipino lad, who, as I have said, was the son of our cook, we set out on what was intended to be a pleasure excursion to Cavité.

Of course, since the war broke out, if not before, every American boy knows that Cavité was the Spanish naval station in Manila Bay, and that the city is the capital of the province known by that same name.

There is a town, a bay, and a peninsula, all of which are called Cavité; but before visiting the place Ray and I believed it was simply a naval station, because those in Manila whose language we could understand referred to it as if there were nothing else of importance to be found there.

Now Panda had a brother who was a fisherman, and who sailed on a boat such as would attract no little attention in Boston Harbour. It was a long, wooden canoe, and the Filipinos call such craft "bancas." It had two masts with sails made of lateen stiffened by bamboo ribs, and a lateen sail looks very much like such a window curtain as I have seen in my great-grandfather's home nearabout Gloucester, formed of thin, narrow strips of what appears to be wood.

Two of these boats work in company, and are fastened together with strips of bamboo, which hold them ten or twelve feet apart, while made fast to the stern of each craft is a scoop-net. It is only a question of sailing here and there wherever the fish are supposed to be found near the surface, and dipping up such as are not frightened away by the approach of the canoes. Not very exciting sport; but Ray and I were certain we should find some amusement in it, when Panda, who, luckily for us, could speak English because of having been employed by my father during such time as he had lived in Manila, explained that we would run down as far as Cavité, staying there all day, perhaps, and returning during the evening.

We knew on leaving Hong Kong that war was about to be declared between the United States and Spain; yet it did not seem reasonable that in these far-off islands we would see any fighting, and it is certain that our father had little idea we might be so decidedly mixed up with the conflict between the two nations as to be in great danger of our lives.

Of the queer-looking and queer-tasting food which we took with us, or of the odd contrivances for fishing which we found on board the bancas, there is no opportunity to speak, for I would come to the end of our adventures in the number of pages which Ray has insisted shall make up the story.

If it so be that some gentleman sees fit to publish it, the lad who reads what I have set down must imagine, by aid of such books as can be borrowed from the Public Library, what sort of an appearance we made on that morning, the last day of April, when we embarked on an excursion which promised a little something in the way of novelty, and introduced us to more actual danger than we are ever likely to see again in the same number of hours, no matter how long it may be permitted us to live.

So far as concerned the fishing, it was neither more nor less than might have been seen in any portion of the world where a net is dragged through the water with the chance of capturing such fish as are near the surface; not exciting sport, nor calculated to give one a desire for more of the same kind.

Ray and I lay idly on our backs upon the bench-like seat in the stern of the banca owned by Panda's brother, gazing curiously at the shore, for to us there was much of interest even in the conformation of that bay wherein so many stirring actions had occurred; but Panda ran to and fro something after the manner of an excited monkey, jabbering in his own language with the crew, as if this skimming the top of the water with a net was a very heroic deed.

Ray, forgetting that we were for the time supposed to be fishermen, recalled to my mind the fact that this archipelago of the Philippines was discovered by Magellan on the twelfth day of March, in the year 1521, and by him named the St. Lazarus Islands. He referred to the severe earthquakes of 1874 and 1880, when, in the last named year, the destruction of property and life in the island of Luzon was fearful.

Having in view the story of our travels, which was nearly completed, he read from a printed slip which we brought with us from Boston the following facts that had been constantly in my mind for the past three months, and may as well be set down here in condensed form for the benefit of those lads who are given to indolence in matters of geography.

" There are thirty-one islands of considerable size in the Philippine group, with eight ports open to commerce. The population is about eight millions, of which more than three millions are in the island of Luzon, the largest of the archipelago, having an area of 40,885 square miles. Manila, the principal city, had as population in 1880 in the walled town 12,000, and in the suburbs from 250,000 to 300,000.

" The city was founded in 1571, and is situated on the eastern shore of a circular bay one hundred and twenty miles in circumference.

" Manila was captured from the Spaniards by the English in 1762, the assaulting forces being led by General William Draper, with Admiral Cornish commanding the naval division. On the twenty-fourth of September the troops were disembarked just south of the city, and the siege continued until the sixth of October, when a breach was effected in the Spanish works, and the town carried by storm. After the surrender the Spanish officials agreed to pay as a ransom for the city two millions of dollars in gold, and the same amount of money in bills on the Treasury at Madrid."

As if considering it necessary to read all the information we had gathered concerning these islands of the Philippines, Ray went further into the history of the group from his store of clippings, and read of what had taken place in this same bay of Manila from the year 1571, when the island of Luzon was reduced to subjection by General Legazpi.

He read of ten attacks which were made within less than four years thereafter by the Chinese, when the battles lasted several days; of the massacre of Chinese in 1603, when 23,000 were murdered, and also that of 1629, when no less than 35,000 were killed in cold blood, to say nothing of the many attacks that were afterward made, when hundreds of the so-called foreigners were put to death.

Then came the story of the latest insurrections in the Philippines, beginning with that headed by Dr. José Rizal, and ending with the one in progress at this day, when we knew, although it seemed like something occurring afar off, that Emilio Aguinaldo, with a following of natives, threatened Manila.

This last fact, however, gave Ray and me no more disquietude than it did Panda, for it was not believed the
insurgents would be able to make much headway against
the Spaniards, unless by chance the American forces
should come to this portion of the world, and whatever
others may have thought, we two lads were quite certain
the Philippines were too far from the United States for
such an event to be probable.

How much more of descriptive matter with which we
were already familiar Ray might have read, I cannot say ;
but he was in the humour to continue, as if wishing to
refresh his own memory, and would have gone on at this
work for some time had we not just then arrived within
a respectful distance of the Spanish fleet.

Since leaving San Francisco we had seen many naval
vessels, but never at so short a range ; and it pleased me
when the fishermen brought the bancas around in order
to empty their nets, with the hope that they might be
able to sell some of the catch.

Ray spelled the names for me to write down, and very
glad indeed did I feel at that moment because this formidable array of war-ships was not where they could make
an attack upon our people.

There was the *Reina Maria Christina*, the *Castilla*,
Velasco, Don Antonio de Ulloa, Don Juan de Austria, and
such small craft as the *General Lezo, El Correo, Marques
del Duero, Isla de Cuba*, and *Isla de Luzon*.

Whether the fishermen had a successful catch or not
it is impossible to say, for by the time I had gotten these

Spanish names written down we were considerably beyond the fleet, and now all the conversation turned to warfare, Panda joining us that he might describe in his peculiar fashion what the insurgent Aguinaldo had done, and what it was believed he yet would do, but to that I gave little heed.

Surely those who had arisen against Spain would not be able to do much mischief roundabout Manila while so large a fleet lay anchored between that city and Cavité, and I put an end to Panda's boasting by declaring, as if I knew all the particulars, that "until the American peo-had given the Spaniards a much needed lesson, there was little chance any insurrection on the island would make very great progress."

"You do not know my people," Panda said, vehemently, and then for the first time I began to feel just a trifle uneasy in mind.

The boy had said that Aguinaldo's force was even then within a short distance of Cavité, and might it not be possible that we should find ourselves between the fire of this Spanish fleet and the insurgents' guns?

I said as much as this to Ray, for Panda, having exhausted his predictions and his threats against the Spaniards, went forward to see the fish that had been taken from the nets.

"It is not probable these half-naked people will be so venturesome as to make an attack anywhere in this bay while it is so well fortified," Ray replied, laughingly. "Look at the forts there at Cavité, and then at the batteries around Manila. If that isn't enough to set your fears at rest, remember that both the islands of Corregidor and Caballo, at the entrance to the bay, are fortified, to say nothing of that point yonder. Why, Ernest Hyde, there is no ordinary fleet of vessels that would dare to enter such a body of water as this, where are planted submarine mines, as father has said, and yet you talk about Aguinaldo's beggarly army, as if believing he would dare make a venture that could end only in defeat, however many there might be who follow him."

All this seemed reasonable, and I put from my mind the faint forebodings of the future, which had come at a time when we seemed most secure, to enjoy the scene around me.

I had almost forgotten there were any insurgents on the island of Luzon, when finally we were come to the landing-place at the suburbs of Cavité, and immediately our bancas were surrounded by a crowd of natives who talked loudly, indulging in many gestures which seemed to me threatening, meanwhile looking at Ray and me from time to time in a manner by no means agreeable.

It is all very well for a fellow to declare that he is brave, but put him where Ray and I were at that moment, with none but natives near at hand ; then surround him with two hundred or more disagreeable-looking fellows who appeared on the point of making an attack upon him, and I venture to say he will feel quite as uncomfortable in mind, however much he prides himself upon his bravery, as did my brother and myself.

Having once given Ray an opportunity to laugh at me because of my fears, I tried hard to hold my tongue while we remained here on the shore, unable to move in either direction because of the half-naked throng which entirely surrounded us, and it was absolutely a relief, oddly as that statement may sound, when my brother displayed signs of fear.

"If this is the sort of company we are likely to have, it would be a good idea to find passage back to Manila in some of the steamers which father has said run to and fro, for I have no desire to spend a day with such companions as these."

"Let us ask Panda to lead us at once to his brother's house," I said, for it was understood when we left home that we should find cleanly and comfortable quarters less than a mile outside the city, with the cook's son, but Panda was too busily engaged with these newly met acquaintances to pay much attention to us until we had called his name loudly several times, when he came up with the air of one who is vexed at being disturbed.

"Why have all these men come here to meet us?" I asked, perhaps a trifle roughly, because, as I have said, there was considerable disquietude in my mind.

He seemingly gave no heed to my roughness of speech; but answered curtly, almost insolently, as I fancied:

"Does it seem strange to American boys that a poor Filipino should be glad to meet his relations?"

"Are all these relatives of yours?" Ray asked, with

a laugh, and it was not a pleasant expression which came over Panda's face as he replied :

."We are all of the same blood, and those who are oppressed by the Spaniards are drawn more closely together, perhaps, than people who live in a free country."

Surely Panda had never talked about oppression, or had very much to say regarding the insurgents, until the moment when we were come within hail of the Spanish

fleet; but now it was as if he had suddenly learned of the wrongs done his people, and was minded to avenge them. At least that was the way I read the decided change in his demeanour, and it was by no means pleasant to find ourselves thus mixed up in what might cause our father trouble with the Spanish officials if it should be made known.

"You shall show us where we can find conveyance back to the city," I said, decidedly. "Ray and I have concluded it will be better to stay at home, than here among people who do not seem friendly disposed."

"They are the same as your brothers," Panda replied, now laying aside somewhat of his insolence. "Surely an American should be a welcome visitor, for it is that country which we believe will free us from Spanish rule."

"If this is the way of showing friendliness, I wonder to what lengths they might go in case of meeting with an enemy," Ray added, with a laugh, and I understood that he was beginning to grow more comfortable in mind.

"The day may come when you shall see that," Panda said, with an ominous shake of the head, and I interrupted him by insisting that he lead us to where we might find a steamer on which we could take passage back to Manila.

"You must go to my brother's house," he replied, much as if we were under his command. "I have told these good friends that the Americans will thus honour us, and you cannot well force me to break my word."

Whether he gave a signal to the throng around us, or they, understanding somewhat of the conversation, acted upon an impulse, I cannot say; but certain it is that Panda had no sooner spoken than we were surrounded in such manner that escape would have been impossible, and immediately every man, Ray and I in the centre of the crowd, moved away from the shore toward what appeared to be a suburb of the town.

CHAPTER II.

IT seemed ridiculous to suppose for a single instant that we were prisoners, and yet it amounted to very much the same thing, since we were literally forced to go whithersoever these excited friends of Panda's chose to direct their steps.

I was not disposed to let Ray know all that was in my mind, fearing lest he would laugh at me for being a coward; but I glanced at him now and then as we were forced through the outskirts of the town toward the country beyond, until coming to understand that he was by no means pleased with the general situation of affairs.

Then I said in what I intended should be a careless tone :

"These people of Cavité are disposed to be very friendly."

"I wish I could think they had no other feeling toward us, Ernest, for just now it seems much as if we had been captured."

"One might think that but for such an idea being ridiculous," I said, sharply, hoping to convince myself in persuading him that there was no danger in the situation.

"Why should the Filipinos, and particularly friends of Panda, have any care concerning us?"

"That is a question which I cannot answer, but would give much to know exactly why they are so careful regarding our welfare. Do you think it would be of any avail if we should make stout resistance just now?"

I glanced quickly around us. At the lowest estimate there were not less than a hundred and fifty who thus forced us along at a pace so rapid that at times we were obliged to break into a run lest we be overthrown.

It would be folly to think of making a stand against them, unless it so chanced they really were in a friendly mood, and in such case I had no desire to make myself ridiculous even in the eyes of a Filipino.

Ray read what was in my mind, and the knowledge of our helplessness aroused him to anger.

"I will soon know what they mean! Panda shall make some kind of an explanation, if it so be he can!"

Then he raised his voice, calling upon the lad by name, and those nearest began gesticulating wildly, pointing repeatedly toward Corregido Island, much as if to say that he who brought us into this snarl had gone in that direction.

Now for the first time I realised that we were indeed alone with these natives to whom the shedding of white men's blood is no real crime, and, despite all efforts to the contrary, my courage oozed away until I was thoroughly alarmed.

During all this time we had been proceeding, as I have

said, at a rapid pace toward the country immediately behind Cavité, and were now well beyond the town.

Ray, no less disturbed than I, began to look about for something in the situation which might appear less dark; but his speculations were not well calculated to relieve my anxiety of mind.

"If there had been any danger in our coming here with Panda, father would have known it, and put a stop to the excursion when it was first mentioned; but yet, if everything is as it should be, why have that miserable little Filipino and his brother suddenly disappeared? Why has this crowd of villainous-looking natives brought us away when it must have been known we counted on going back to Manila?"

As a matter of course I could not answer these questions. For a moment came the thought that I would force the affair to an issue by refusing to go a single step farther.

Then, when I made as if to halt, those in the rear pushed me forward roughly, and yet with every indication of mirth.

It was a singular situation, to say the least, and would have puzzled many an older and brighter lad than myself.

If the excursion had been arranged several days in advance, it might seem as if this were a scheme to take us prisoners for some especial purpose. Perhaps that we might be held for ransom, or to force our father, one of the leading American residents in Manila, to use his

influence in favour of Aguinaldo's plans. But from the moment we had decided to go, until embarking on the banca, Panda had not so much as left our dwelling.

Puzzle over it as we might, the only certainty about the situation was that we must, for the time being, do whatsoever those who virtually held us prisoners commanded, for we had seen no white man to whom an appeal could be made, and even though we met one it was doubtful if, in case this throng of Filipinos permitted an interview, we should be able to make ourselves understood, because neither Ray nor I spoke Spanish.

As we advanced more slowly now that we were clear of the town, men left the throng to run hurriedly back, while others joined us with what was evidently important and pleasing information. Their movements reminded me of a swarm of bees, and the sound of their conversation was not unlike the buzzing of these insects when they set out in search of a new home.

During fully half an hour we were urged forward, and then the party had arrived at the bank of a small, swiftly running brook, on either side of which could be seen crops of hemp or groves of cocoa palms, while directly in front one might look through the narrow pathway of green cut in the foliage, until he saw the mountains beyond.

A short distance from where we had halted were several dwellings with thatches of nipa palm ; but for the time being these appeared to have no occupants, and none of our captors made any attempt at entering them.

The Filipinos squatted down by the side of the brook,

still talking loudly and without paying any apparent attention to us; but I was quick to note the fact that we
were surrounded, although not quite so closely as when
we were forced to make the journey from the shore.

The men fell back with a sort of respectful manner,
leaving us comparatively alone; but they took good care
to form a circle completely around us, so that any attempt
at escape — I use the word because in my mind there was
no question but that we were prisoners — would have been
absolutely in vain.

In view of the wonderful things we saw shortly afterward, and the many dangers which beset us, the time
spent here amid the Filipinos seems now to be but a
trifling matter, but yet at the moment it appeared most
serious.

Therefore it is that I will say no more concerning our
fears and forebodings, nor set down that which we said
one to another, for both of us believed our lives were in
peril.

We finally solved the matter in our own minds, and
then came a decided sense of relief at being able, as we
believed, to penetrate the mystery, by deciding that
we were really prisoners, to be held until father could
effect our release by ransom, or whatsoever else it was the
natives were eager to obtain.

We were given food and fruit in plentiful abundance;
no one ventured to come nigh us, save in order to bring
something which we might need, and thus did we remain
until sunset, when, to our great surprise and yet greater

relief, Panda and his brother, in company with half a dozen others, came up.

Immediately I began to reproach the miserable Filipino lad for his treachery; but there was on his mind something of such vast importance that he gave no heed to the angry words which sprang to my lips.

"We must not go back to Manila until morning, and perhaps not then," he said, excitedly, while those who accompanied him were talking vehemently to their acquaintances.

"Why do you say that we must not go back?" I cried, in anger. "Do you believe it possible that we can thus be spirited away, and without danger to yourself? You shall pay for this outrage with your liberty."

Panda looked at me in mute astonishment, and I knew full well that the expression on his face could not have been assumed.

"Have you been treated ill?" he asked, solicitously.

"What else can you call it, when we are thus held prisoners?"

Panda looked around him as if asking what might have happened during his absence, and Ray, shaking him by the arm, said, hotly:

"Do not think to deceive us by such a show of ignorance! We were forced to come to this place, as you know full well, when it was our desire to go back to Manila."

"But you cannot go back, señor," the boy said, quite innocently. "It is not safe when the American war-vessels may sail into the bay at any moment. Why not remain here until the fight is ended?"

"What fight?" I asked, now thoroughly bewildered, and after many an attempt to hit upon the right word to express his meaning, Panda finally told a story which seemed to me, at the moment, to be positively incredible.

It would be useless to make any attempt at repeating it after his fashion, for many times was it necessary to go over certain statements several times, that we might come at the true meaning; but in substance, this was the marvellous tale he told :

Word had been brought by some of the insurgents that an American fleet was rapidly approaching Manila Bay, and, since war was declared between Spain and the United States, there could be no question as to the purpose of these naval vessels in coming this way.

So nearly as we could gather, this information had been kept a profound secret by the Filipinos lest the Spaniards, getting wind of the intended attack, should be prepared. The insurgents' great hope was that the Americans would win a decided victory, and thus give them liberty.

Panda had even more important news to tell, or, at least, so it seemed to him, for his people stoutly affirmed that no less a person than Aguinaldo himself would be on board one of the vessels to pilot the fleet into the bay.

Try as we might, it was impossible to get a clear idea of how this startling information had been received. One version of his story was that some fishermen, sighting the squadron, had paddled with all speed to Cavité, and there told those who were known to be true to the cause of freedom of the great deliverance which was apparently at hand. Then again he spoke of runners, coming over land, who had seen the vessels off Point Subic, but whether the information had been brought by one or both of these messengers, we could not determine.

At all events, Panda was certain that within a very few hours, perhaps before we could return to Manila, the American squadron would enter the bay, and now that this explanation had been made, we could well understand the excitement which prevailed among those who had escorted us hither.

After the lad told the news, I demanded to know why his people had made us prisoners, and he gave such explanation as seemed satisfactory, — an explanation which I doubted not was the truth.

With his brother and four or five others he had been sent along the shore to warn the insurgents, for it seemed that these humble fishermen were leagued with those who would throw off the yoke of Spain, even as we of the United States had thrown off that of the British. His departure was necessarily hurried, and he, thinking to return within an hour, charged those nearest at hand that special care be taken of Ray and myself.

The Filipinos, believing a desperate battle was about to be fought, perhaps within a very short time, and knowing that Cavité, as the naval station, would be one of the points of attack, had simply sought safety in this secluded retreat, bringing us with them apparently by force, because of their inability to explain why it seemed necessary we should accompany them.

Now, as I have since learned, there had been much talk in Manila concerning the possibility that the city might be attacked, and my father regretted sorely having sent for his family; but once they were arrived, he kept all such information from them, believing there was no good reason why my mother should be alarmed because of what might perhaps be only idle rumour.

Had Panda told his story to my father, it would have been believed at once; but to Ray and me, who had heard of the war only in a general way, and, being taken up with the novelty of the journey, had given but little heed to the statements, the information given by the Filipino seemed incredible.

However, here we were half an hour's tramp from Cavité, and the night had already come.

Unless Panda or his brother could be persuaded to return with us, there seemed little chance we would find our way back without some mishap, unable as we were to speak the language of the country.

From this point of view, it appeared best we should remain quietly where we were until morning; but, knowing how great must be our parents' anxiety, for it was supposed we would return before nightfall, it seemed absolutely wicked for us to thus delay.

Both Ray and I urged this upon the Filipino lad, demanding that he go with us as guide; but he, magnifying the dangers, as I believed then, stoutly refused, declaring it was necessary for our own safety that we remain with his friends, who, as he said, would keep us from all harm.

The boy's story had been interrupted from time to time by those around us, who appealed to him for information concerning the force at Manila, or regarding messages sent by their insurgent friends along the shore, and thus, in addition to the difficulty of understanding all he said, was the tale delayed in the telling fully two hours.

Half as much more time was spent in trying to persuade him to go back with us, and then it was so late that, even had we agreed, we questioned whether transportation might be readily procured.

"There is no other way for us than to stay where we are," Ray said, at length. "It will soon be daylight, and we'll get back as best we can, leaving Panda and his friends to recover from the shock which this news seems to have given them."

There was no other conclusion to be arrived at, and we strove to make ourselves as comfortable as possible, by putting resolutely from our minds all thoughts concerning the anxiety from which our parents must be suffering because of our absence.

After a time, and while the Filipinos were discussing the position of affairs as excitedly as ever, we two fell asleep, lying there by the side of the brook, and it seemed as if my eyes had but just closed in slumber when we were aroused by Panda.

"Our friends have decided that we shall go back to Cavité," he said, in a matter-of-fact tone, as if Ray and I could have no voice in the matter.

"If it was so dangerous to remain there at nightfall, why should you do such a thing?" I asked. "Has it suddenly been discovered that the American fleet is not near the port?"

"There is no thought of going into the city, señor. We will make our way to the high land just beyond, and there it will be possible to see General Aguinaldo when he shows the enemies of Spain how they may advance to victory."

"You won't see your general near the American fleet. If there is any idea of going back to Manila, we'll start; otherwise, I count on finishing my nap," and Ray laid himself down again as if determined to remain where he was.

At these words Panda showed great alarm, and began to talk rapidly in a mixture of Spanish and English, until he would have been good at language who could have understood the purport of his words.

Then Panda's brother, hearing what must have sounded

much like an altercation, came up and added his entreaties, until Ray cried, petulantly :

"Very well, we'll go with you, for there's little chance of my falling asleep again after such a row."

The remainder of the throng, and it seemed to me that the number had been increased very sensibly since we lay down to sleep, came forward with a rush, forcing us onward as they had when we believed ourselves prisoners.

At a violent pace were we swept onward by this living tide, until finding ourselves upon the brow of a slight elevation, half a mile or more beyond Cavité, where could be had an unobstructed view of the city and the entrance to the bay.

Tired from much walking, and fretted by loss of sleep, Ray and I decided that all this excitement, which must have occasioned our parents great anxiety, had no foundation in fact. The story of an American fleet coming into Manila Bay had been invented by some of the insurgents to bolster up the weak-kneed ones in that city, and it was folly for us to put any faith in it.

"I am going to lie down here, and if you are awakened when day breaks, rouse me; we'll start for home as soon as there is a hope of finding our way," Ray said, as he lay down upon the ground, while the throng of natives squatted here and there in such position as would give them the best opportunity for looking out over the waters.

I would have followed my brother's example, but by

this time all desire for slumber had left my eyelids, and
I crouched by his side, involuntarily looking seaward,
although positive nothing of importance would be seen
in that quarter.

It was when the silence seemed most profound that
a great shout went up from those around me, and in an
instant that hilltop was covered with dancing, screaming
beings, while I gazed around in bewilderment.

The noise awakened Ray, and as he leaped to his feet
in alarm, Panda ran up, throwing his arms around our
necks as he screamed incoherent words, at the same time
pointing seaward.

Then, far away in the distance, we saw tiny flashes of
light at brief intervals, and heard a faint rumbling as if
of thunder.

"Can it be possible that our ships are really coming
into the bay?" Ray asked, as soon as we could shake off
Panda and stand face to face.

There was no question but that heavy guns were being
discharged far away in the vicinity of Corregidor, and
I believe the time never passed so slowly to any one as
it did to us two lads, who stood there on the brow of the
hill amid that throng of excited Filipinos, waiting for the
day to break.

Now and then, when the cries of the men died away
for an instant, I fancied I heard the thud, thud of a
steamer's screw upon the water, but yet not a light could
be seen.

If an attack was about to be made on the Spaniards,

our people would try to steal quietly into the bay, and as this thought came to me I glanced toward the right, down at the quiet city of Cavité.

Then it was I understood that we upon the hilltop were not the only ones who believed a fleet of war-vessels was advancing with deadly intent.

The *Reina Christina*, on board of which we knew was the Spanish admiral, lay just off the arsenal, and astern of her was the *Castilla*. This much I remembered full well, and now as I looked at these two vessels in particular, giving but little heed to the others which lay farther outside, I saw lights flash here and there along their decks, sparks coming from their smoke-stacks, and heard the clanking of iron cables as if the anchors were being raised.

There was no longer any doubt in my mind as to the truth of Panda's story.

The Americans were come into Manila Bay, incredible though that had seemed, and my heart sank within me, because in my ignorance I believed it would be impossible for any fleet of vessels to capture a place so well fortified as was the city of Manila.

It must have been that Ray had thoughts similar to mine, for he said, almost in a whisper, as we stood watching the lights dance to and fro upon the Spanish vessels :

" If there is to be a battle here, and our people are defeated, what will become of the few Americans in Manila ? "

" We won't think of anything like that," I replied,

speaking as bravely as was possible. "We should be able to whip the Spanish fleet."

"And that done, what of the forts? Do you believe they can be taken?"

I made no reply, and he failed to notice the fact, for just then we saw that they were astir on the other ships; we could hear the sound of oars, and fancied it was possible to distinguish the outlines of small boats as they sped to and fro from one vessel to the other.

Then we looked seaward again; but nothing met our gaze, and I failed to hear even that faint noise which we had believed might be the churning of a steamer's screw.

Had our people gone back, or was it all a fancy, in which the Spaniards were tricked as well as ourselves?

It seemed as if I ceased to breathe, save at rare intervals, during the next hour, and then, suddenly, as is the case in the tropics, the light of day flashed out.

In two or three minutes, where had been darkness, was that gray mist which tells of the sun's coming, and a moment later the waters of the bay were lighted up.

Now it was that Ray and I cried quite as loudly and quite as wildly as did the Filipinos, for we saw, seemingly very near the shore, although perhaps it may have been five or six miles away, a noble fleet of mighty ships, from each of which could be seen floating the stars and stripes.

As we afterward came to know, the one nearest at hand was Commodore Dewey's flag-ship, the *Olympia*, then the *Baltimore*, the *Raleigh*, the *Petrel*, the *Concord*, the *Boston*, and lastly the revenue cutter *McCulloch*.

"Aguinaldo! Aguinaldo!" went up from full two hundred throats, and I saw on the bridge of the commodore's vessel a figure smaller than those around him, who may have been, for aught I know, the insurgent leader; but at the time I gave no heed to those tiny specks which represented men, for before us were the vessels of my own country, come, as I then foolishly believed, to meet destruction in an enemy's waters.

And after that destruction, what might be the fate of my father's family?

CHAPTER III.

IT was a glorious sight which we saw from that hill just
beyond Cavité on the morning of the first day of May,
and the lad who has never been in a foreign country fails
to realise what a thrill comes upon him when he sees flying
from the masthead of a ship the star-spangled banner.

If one flag will awaken enthusiasm, fancy what unspeak-
able sensations must have come upon Ray and me as we
saw our flags upon all those noble ships which advanced
as if disdainful of such an enemy as they were about
to meet.

It was no longer possible for me to unite with the
Filipinos in shouts of joy; there was in my heart such
a fear for what the future might bring, as held me silent
and motionless.

It would be impossible for a lad like me to describe in
any fitting way that which followed, when the greatest
naval victory the world ever knew was won before
noon.

I can only write of what I saw, without attempting
to describe the emotions which were awakened by the
scene, and leave to the reader, if it so chance there

be a reader of these lines outside of my own family, to imagine how we two Boston boys must have felt during that forenoon in May.

To witness a naval engagement, when the spectator has no interest whatsoever in either force, cannot fail of being thrilling ; but it passes beyond words when he who looks on believes that the lives of those dear to him, as well as his own, depend upon the result.

Our vessels were drawn out in line, heading straight up the bay as if to pass Cavité and the Spanish fleet without giving any heed to them whatsoever.

Below us, almost at our feet, the enemy's vessels were steaming slowly to and fro like fighters who await an opportunity to gain some slight advantage in the first grapple, and even the Filipinos were awed into silence by the view of these mighty war-machines making ready to go into action.

Our vessels were moving slowly, as if courting an attack, when suddenly, with a boom and a roar that

caused me to start in alarm, came the report of a gun
from the arsenal.

We on the hillside could see the enormous shot as it
sped its way through the air, and I gripped my hands
hard until my finger-nails were pressed into the flesh,
expecting to see the missile crash into one of those
gallant craft whereon floated the stars and stripes.

It fell far astern of the *Boston*, as if to show how
poorly the Spaniards could aim.

Then came another roar, and it was as if the hill on
which we were standing trembled ; a huge volume of
smoke went up, and we knew a second gun had been
discharged.

Yet there was no answer from our vessels, and Ray,
clutching me by the arm with a force which left the
imprints of his fingers for more than two days after,
cried, nervously :

" Why don't they fire ? Our ships will be destroyed
without having done the enemy any damage ! "

He had no more than spoken when a line, made up of
tiny specks of colour, was strung aloft from the *Olympia*,
and, although knowing but little regarding warfare, we
two understood that the commodore was giving some
order to the other vessels of the fleet.

Now we expected to see the flame and smoke belch
forth from those mighty ships, and yet they steamed on
quietly and silently as if their mission were simply to gain
an anchorage off Manila.

Ahead of them, from the direction of the city, came

shot after shot, and the Spanish fleet was hidden in a cloud of smoke as they added to the shower of missiles.

The ground trembled as if smitten by an earthquake, and the roar and rumble of guns was deafening; but yet our fleet steamed straight ahead, with nothing to show that there was life on board, save those bits of colour on the *Olympia*, the commodore's flag, and the glorious stars and stripes.

On they steamed without quickening the pace, but bearing slightly to the left, the Spanish line all aflame from Cavité to Manila, and yet, so far as we could see, not one of all those shots struck its target.

During five minutes or more it appeared to Ray and me as if the Americans were bent on gaining the opposite shore of the bay out of range; as if, after viewing the fortifications and the enemy's fleet, they would retreat, understanding that defeat must follow an attack, and I believe the tears came into my eyes as this thought formed itself in my mind.

We were standing, Ray and I, with clasped hands, and around us were the Filipinos, now suddenly grown silent because it seemed as if the Americans flinched from the combat, when I saw the prow of the *Olympia* turn slightly shoreward. Nearer and nearer on the arc of a circle she bent, until the entire line of vessels was rounding to opposite Manila.

Then it was that Ray and I shouted more loudly than any Filipino could have done, for the battle was on !

Our people were not to be provoked into opening fire until they had made ready, and were in such position as best pleased them. This evidence of cool bravery sent the blood bounding through my veins, and from that moment I ceased to fear the result.

It had seemed certain that the Americans, disregarding the Spanish fleet, counted on opening fire upon Manila, and yet the fleet was swung into line again, heading straight for Cavité without a shot having been fired from the Yankee guns.

Then, and before the battle had opened on our side, occurred what at the moment seemed to me like a strange thing.

Directly in front of the second ship, which was the *Baltimore*, a huge column of water shot up, rising to twice the height of her short masts, and the thunder of the guns was drowned by the rumbling roar which seemed to come from the very bottom of the bay.

Then, and even while we were trying to decide what had caused that sudden up-shooting of the waves, there was another spouting of water, — another shock as if the earth itself had come in contact with some heavier body, and it appeared to us on shore as if the waves dashed directly over the third vessel in line.

"The torpedoes!" Panda shouted. "It is said there are many of them between Manila and Cavité."

Surely the Spaniards, with their batteries, fleet, forts, and submarine torpedoes, should be able to beat off that slender line of vessels which had come so far to avenge

the dastardly deed that had been perpetrated in the harbour of Havana.

To us on shore it was as if the vessels carrying the stars and stripes were close upon Cavité before any sign was made that they proposed to notice the Spanish fleet.

At this time every battery along the shore, so far as we could see, was hurling shot and shell at the American line, which was advancing as if bent only upon a voyage of sightseeing.

Then, and while the Filipinos were shouting words which I could not understand, but believed they expressed impatience or anger because of the delay, from the forward part of the *Olympia* came a jet of smoke, a tongue of fire, and I distinctly saw an iron missile strike the aftermost part of the *Castilla*, ploughing its way through the deck as if through so much paper.

At the same instant another line of fluttering flags went up on the commodore's vessel, and they had no more than been flung out by the breeze before great clouds of smoke arose from our fleet, and we heard the pounding of shot against the hulls of the enemy's vessels even above the roar of those thundering guns.

Now the Filipinos' cries of impatience and anger were suddenly changed to shouts of rejoicing, in which Ray and I joined without really being conscious of what we were doing.

The battle was on, and, however much damage might have been inflicted upon our ships, of a certainty the enemy was getting a punishment so terrifying that they could not long withstand it.

Now and then, as the clouds of smoke lifted, I counted the leaden-coloured hulls, fearing lest one or another — perhaps all — had been sunk by that furious rain of iron which came from the shore and the Spanish vessels; yet each time I did so the number was complete.

There was no sign of disaster, no increase of speed, nor lessening of it. All, so far as the manœuvre was concerned, remained the same as when we first saw the squadron.

Would that I could describe the spectacle so that he who reads might see it in his mind's eye, as our fleet steamed past Cavité Point, circling to the right only a mile or more beyond, and coming down again in line of battle, dealing death and destruction at every discharge of the rapidly served guns.

The morning was blazing hot; but we on shore heeded it not. Now and then a missile, as like from one fleet as the other, would strike within five hundred yards of where we stood; but it caused us no alarm.

We had ceased to have any other sense than that of sight. Personal discomfort was entirely forgotten. The heat and the mental strain caused the perspiration to run down my face in tiny streams, and I was conscious of it only because my eyes were suffused with moisture.

We had lost sight of town and of ship and of battery, in the sulphurous smoke which hung over all, when the cloud was wafted aside by a gentle breeze from the shore,

and we saw two small steamers putting out from the shore at full speed, heading directly for the American flag-ship.

I wondered if they were carrying a message from the Spanish admiral, when Ray shouted in my ear:

"They are torpedo-boats! They are torpedo-boats, and in the smoke our people will fail to see them!"

Again it was as if my heart literally stood still, — as if my breath ceased to come because of the fear which beset me that his words might prove true.

Then suddenly, almost at the same instant the terror had come upon me, I saw one of the little craft disappear beneath the waves as if forced down by some giant hand. The other, turning swiftly, while the black smoke which poured out of her stack evidenced the frantic efforts of her firemen, headed for the shore, eager to escape that murderous rain of shot and shell which had destroyed her companion.

The smoke shut down once more, and when it lifted again we saw a Spanish shot strike the second vessel in the line, the *Baltimore*, fairly on her side, and disappear within the iron armour.

It was when the ships were steaming back toward Manila again that this was done, and from the Filipinos, as well as us two American boys, a cry of horror burst forth.

But no more than five minutes later we saw her again, apparently uninjured, and doing as much execution in the fight as either of the other vessels.

Until our people came back past Cavité again the Spanish fleet remained close inshore, moving slowly back and forth, but evidently taking good care not to increase the distance from the land, and then it was that the *Reina Christina* went swiftly out toward the *Olympia* as if challenging her to a duel.

And the challenge was accepted.

It seemed to me as if I had no more than time to count a hundred before the enemy's flag-ship was steaming back at full speed to get under the shelter of Cavité Point, while the flames were bursting out from her stern.

"The Spaniards are getting the worst of it all along the line, and our people appear to be as bright and smiling as ever," Ray yelled in my ear, apparently unable to remain silent any longer.

The smoke settled down again ; the roar of the guns and the tremor of the earth seemed to have increased. The very air quivered under the terrifying concussions, and while enveloped in this cloud, American and Spaniard, from vessel and fort and battery, did their full part in the horrible din.

It seemed to me as if a very long time passed during which we saw nothing and heard nothing distinctly, because the heavy thundering had destroyed our sense of hearing, and then I realised that the noise had abated.

It became less and less until finally ceasing entirely, and we on the shore anxiously asked ourselves who had come off conquerors in this battle, wherein it seemed as if the odds were heavily against the Americans.

Gradually the smoke lifted, and we saw, to our surprise and consternation, those vessels flying the American flag headed directly for the opposite shore of the bay as if in full retreat.

I looked around about me, and at that moment felt a certain sense of affection for those Filipinos, whom, a few hours before, I had considered my enemies, for on the face of each was written deepest sorrow.

They also believed the battle was lost, and we stood staring after that retreating line of noble vessels, not one of whom appeared to have received serious injury, until Panda burst forth in a perfect explosion of noise.

He was dancing to and fro on the hill, as if unable to remain quiet a single moment, and pointing with both hands at the enemy's fleet below us.

Lying close under Cavité Point was the *Reina Christina*, the black smoke pouring up from her decks telling of the enemy which she had within her hull. The *Castilla* appeared to be in flames from stem to stern, and one of the other vessels, the *Velasco*, I afterward came to believe it was, gave good evidence that she would soon be destroyed.

Every vessel in our fleet was steaming away in much the same order and at the same pace as when she entered the bay, while no less than three of the Spaniards were the same as destroyed, and I asked myself, involuntarily speaking aloud, why our people were running away.

It was a question none of us could answer, and for ten minutes or more we stood there in a most singular frame of mind.

On one hand was that which caused us keenest satis
faction and joy, — not because of the loss of human life,
but that our people had whipped their enemy.   On
the other hand we saw the stars and stripes in what
seemed like full retreat, and we were gladdened and
perplexed, and sorrowful and wondering, all at the same
instant.

While we stood there in a maze of bewilderment the
flames burst out from the *Isla de Cuba*, and on nearly all
the other vessels in Cavité Bay were the men running to
and fro as if in dire distress.

We had fresh cause for wonderment when our fleet,
steaming slowly around, came to a standstill opposite the
city, but so far away that, so far as fighting was concerned,
it might as well have been at the other end of the bay.

There the vessels remained silent and menacing, as if
having steamed off simply to watch the work of destruction which was being continued even after they had
withdrawn from the fight.

After a time — perhaps half an hour — we came to
understand, or believed we did, that our fleet had simply
retired to allow the flames opportunity to complete the
work they had so well begun, and once this satisfactory
idea gained lodgment in our minds we were able to speak
with some degree of calmness concerning the wondrous
spectacle which had been witnessed.

The Filipinos were literally wild with delight.   They
knew beyond a question that, if the Spanish fleet had not
been absolutely destroyed, it was so far disabled as to be

virtually out of the fight, and the victory was with the Americans.

To a man they insisted that Aguinaldo himself was on the bridge of the *Olympia* when she first steamed past Cavité, and equally positive were they that freedom from

foreign rule was near at hand for the inhabitants of the island.

Ray and I had a very good idea as to how lively was their sense of thankfulness, when each in turn insisted upon embracing us, simply because we had come from the United States, and before that time of hugging was at an end we knew that the noise and smoke of battle had not deprived us of all our senses.

The evidences of disaster to the enemy increased each

moment, until before the end of an hour I think no less than five vessels were in flames to a greater or less degree, and the forts and water batteries showed signs of much suffering from Yankee shot and Yankee shell.

Several of the more venturesome among our Filipino companions would have advanced nearer the city, bent, evidently, upon some concerted plan, of which Panda professed himself to be in ignorance; but the cooler heads pointed to the war-vessels lying just beyond range, suggesting, with apparently good reason, that there might be more fighting in the vicinity of Cavité Point.

As for Ray and myself, we had no desire to approach nearer the enemy, feeling quite certain that if we showed ourselves to the Spanish soldiery just at this time we might receive exceedingly rough handling. We no longer felt that our parents were in great anxiety concerning us, for surely now the cause of our delay must be in some slight degree understood, although it was reasonable to suppose father would fail to guess exactly why we had not returned home early the previous afternoon, and it seemed in every way wisest and safest to remain on the hill until the Spaniards were more thoroughly beaten than at that time was evident.

How the moments dragged after we had settled in our own minds the precise condition of affairs on both sides! How eagerly we gazed at the American vessels for some signs of their return, and how keenly we watched the enemy's ships lest one or more of them should make an attempt at escape!

It seemed to me as if one whole day passed while we remained inactive there, looking out over that terrible picture, and then it was with a sense of deepest relief, as if some terrible time of trial and suffering were about to be brought to an end, that I saw the ships, which had been lying in wait, begin to move toward us once more.

I think at this moment black smoke was pouring up from no less than four of the Spanish fleet, and it seemed much like striking a man after he was down, to pour shot and shell into those disabled vessels; but it was necessary because the royal flag was still flying — because they did not choose to acknowledge themselves beaten when they were well-nigh destroyed.

Steadily our vessels advanced, and this time the enemy was not eager to renew the conflict.

Commodore Dewey's fleet steamed gradually up into position, opening fire with such precision that we could distinctly see the first half-dozen shots as they fell upon the uninjured of those vessels lying in Cavité Bay.

Then the smoke of battle covered everything once more.

The thunder of the guns drowned all other noise, and the tremor in the air caused one to experience a sensation of giddiness.

It was noontime. The heat was so intense as to be painful to us on the hillside.

There was no breath of air stirring, and one could well imagine what must be the sufferings of those gallant lads

confined between walls of iron, heated inside by the fires
of the furnaces and the discharges of the guns until such
a temperature as caused us suffering was like unto cool
air.

Before the cloud of wool-like vapour shut out the fleet
from view, we saw the *Baltimore* standing well in toward
the shore to begin a deliberate attack upon the fortifications on Cavité Point, stopping after the first discharge
to pour a broadside into the *Reina Christina* that seemed
literally to blow her to fragments.

Some one farther down the hill passed back the word
— for one could not shout with any hope of being heard
a yard away — that the *San Juan de Austria* was sunk,
and after that we saw no more until the firing ceased.

This time we did not suffer from suspense as before,
for we knew beyond a question that all the Spanish
vessels and fortifications were disabled or had surrendered, and we waited with more of curiosity than of
eagerness to learn which it might be.

What we saw when the clouds of smoke passed away
was almost appalling.

The forts and batteries within our range of vision were
silenced, and where the Spanish fleet had floated so
proudly only a few hours before, there was nothing but
blackened hulls, half submerged or beached upon the
shore.

Three vessels were missing, and we knew they had
been sunk. Eight were quite or nearly consumed by the
flames, and a number of small craft which had plied be-

tween Manila and Cavité were following in the wake of our fleet, flying American instead of Spanish flags.

As for our vessels, they were steaming in the direction of Manila, with the exception of one which was yet behind the point pouring shot into two or three small gunboats that were huddled together in shallow water as if for mutual protection.

I gave little heed to this last work, so deeply was I interested in the further manœuvres of our ships, and, as might have been expected, we presently saw them come to anchor off the city of Manila.

As for the town and arsenal of Cavité, they were still in the possession of the enemy; but that seemed at the moment of small importance, for we knew they could be captured whenever Commodore Dewey was minded to go back to his work.

It was at this time, while the Filipinos were given up to a delirium of triumph and joy, that Ray and I mutely questioned each other as to what we should do.

Under the present condition of affairs, while the American fleet lay off the city, it was not probable we would be allowed to enter, for unquestionably the Spanish troops were guarding it as closely as might be.

This also was the case with the city at our feet, and there seemed to be no choice left us but to remain with our Filipino companions, sharing such quarters as they might be able to provide us with.

I do not think either Ray or I spoke while we stood facing each other with such thoughts in our minds. It was as if I could read readily the perplexities which beset him, and he was not at a loss to understand me.

It was Panda who settled the matter for us by coming up excitedly as he embraced us once more, crying, in a tone of deepest affection :

"The Americans and the Filipinos are brothers! You shall remain with my people until the red, white, and blue flag is hoisted over Manila. We will care for you as we would for our best beloved, for it is your people who have given us freedom!"

CHAPTER IV

IT was all very well for Panda to talk about the Filipinos being our brothers, and that sort of thing, but it
did not go far toward relieving our minds.

To the right of us, and directly below on the shore,
we could see the Spanish flags still flying. The inhabitants of both cities were shut in until it should please the
military authorities to allow them to depart, and we were
shut out.

No one could say how long a time might elapse before
we could be with our parents again, and it was this fact
which dampened the joy that had come to us at the
moment of victory.

The longer I thought of the situation the more unpleasant, even dangerous, did our position appear, until I was
resolved to put it out of my mind for the time being, and
I said to Ray, with as much of cheerfulness as it was
possible to assume :

"Since we cannot mend matters, there is no good
reason why we should borrow trouble by imagining that
all sorts of evil must come upon us. Father will surely
find some means of communicating with the commander

of our fleet, and before many hours have passed we shall
see him."

"That might be true. if he knew exactly where to find
us ; but how is it possible for him to learn that we are
skulking in the hills back of Cavité, or how may he send
a message to us while the Spaniards hold possession of
the shore ? "

"Both cities must be surrendered before a great while,
now that the fleet has been destroyed," I replied, trying
to make what seemed very dark to me appear bright
to him.

Then Panda interfered, and it was well he did, for we
had almost forgotten the glorious victory in our own personal troubles. Had we been left alone a few moments
more both of us would have been plunged into utter
despair.

The Filipinos were making ready to approach the city,
confident that the insurgents would be nearabout await-
ing the landing of their leader, for, as I have said, every
one was confident Aguinaldo had entered the bay on board
the American fleet.

Panda insisted, with somewhat of authority in his tone,
that we accompany the throng, and indeed there seemed to
be no other course for us to pursue. To separate ourselves
from those who were willing to give us shelter and food
would, at this time, have been little less than folly, and
I was determined to appear brave even while I felt
cowardly.

"We will go with Panda," I said to Ray, "and forget,

so far as possible, all disagreeable matters. Neither our parents nor ourselves are in any danger — "

"How can you say that?" my brother asked, bitterly. "After what our vessels have done this day, do you believe the life of an American is safe?"

"Who would do them harm?" I asked, stoutly, but with an inward tremor, for a yet greater fear suddenly came upon me. "Surely the natives will be friendly, and if the lower classes of Spaniards in the city should attempt to commit murder, the English would take sides with the Americans."

It was well this discussion was not allowed to proceed further, else might we have worked ourselves into such a frame of mind as would have unfitted us for that which followed, when it became necessary we be keenly alive to all the surroundings.

Panda's friends were eager to approach the city, and not disposed to spend much time in persuading us to accompany them. In fact, the Filipino lad himself, growing impatient because of the delay, plumply told us that we must set out with him at once, or go our way without further expectation of assistance or guidance from him.

The victory, which these natives believed would be of such wondrous benefit to their cause, made them all exceedingly valiant, and just at this time their General Aguinaldo was a greater man than the American Commodore Dewey.

Ray and I followed the party down the hillside, and then along the plain until we had come to the suburbs of

the city, when the majority of them halted while a few
went forward to reconnoitre, for there were too many
Spanish soldiers in and about Cavité, every one of whom
was probably in a bad humour, to render it safe for a party
of insurgent sympathisers to show themselves boldly.

We had halted under the shade of a nipa-thatched ware
house, and there the party remained upwards of an hour
before any of the scouts returned.

The arsenal, the navy yard, and the water batteries on
the point were yet in possession of the king's forces, so
the spies reported, and it would be in the highest degree
unsafe to enter the city until the Americans should complete their work.

As a matter of course there was no possibility we might
get transportation to Manila, even had we been disposed
to run the risks of the short passage, and with such good
grace as could be called up we submitted ourselves to the
inevitable. In other words, we bowed to the fact that

we must remain away from our parents for at least twenty-four hours longer.

Had we been less troubled in mind, this delay would not have seemed unpleasant, because of what was occurring around us.

The insurgents and their friends had begun to gather in expectation of seeing Aguinaldo ; and the disaffected natives joined the rapidly increasing throng from motives of curiosity or policy, for now had come the time when they must declare for or against those who styled themselves patriots.

We came down from the hillside perhaps two hundred strong, and in less than an hour after arriving at the warehouse I believe there were more than a thousand in the immediate vicinity.

At first we saw weapons in the hands of a few ; but as night approached nearly every man armed himself after some fashion or other, until the throng presented a most formidable appearance.

Even Panda, boy that he was, carried a sword-like knife, and would have pressed upon us something of the same kind but that we refused to accept arms of any sort.

"Weapons would be of but little use to us, either against these people or the Spanish soldiers, and we are safer while defenceless," Ray whispered to me when the party began to take on a warlike appearance.

I was of the same opinion, and therefore did we refuse Panda's offer.

There was no lack of food. The people nearabout, and

even for several miles back in the country, rejoicing because of the downfall of their ancient enemy, brought out all their stores, and had Aguinaldo appeared then he would have found at his call a full regiment of armed men, provisioned for two or three days.

Until late in the night Ray and I spent the time in watching these people, but understanding not a word that was said, and seeing Panda only at rare intervals.

The cook's son had suddenly become a person of importance, in his own eyes at least, and gave but little heed to us.

We were not troubled by his neglect for the time being ; but promised each other that we would keep a watchful eye on him next morning, so that he should be forced to act as guide. It seemed probable that then we might succeed in getting into Manila, for I believed the city would speedily surrender to Commodore Dewey after such an exhibition of his power as had just been given.

We remained in the warehouse all night, for the very good reason that there was no other convenient place near at hand, and slept as best we could while a thousand or more natives moved restlessly to and fro, brandishing weapons and giving vent to what we believed were threats against the government which had so long held them in subjection.

With the first light of dawn Ray and I were where we could command a view of the bay in the direction of Manila, and to our great relief we saw one of Commodore Dewey's vessels get under way and steam toward us.

Now was come the time, as we believed, when all our troubles would be speedily ended, but we were not so fortunate.

It was the *Baltimore*, as we afterward learned, which had left her anchorage, and, instead of stopping at Cavité even long enough to throw a shot or shell into the fortifications, she steamed directly past us in the direction of Corregidor, and more than one of the natives believed she was leaving the bay to summon assistance.

" Our people will give no attention to Cavité until after Manila has surrendered," Ray said, despondently, and I was of the same mind until a few moments later, when we saw another vessel leave her anchorage to come in our direction.

It was the *Petrel*, and the fear flashed upon me that all of the squadron would leave us ; that the destruction of the Spanish fleet was Commodore Dewey's only purpose in visiting the bay, and, the task having been accomplished, he was about to return to his former rendezvous.

This time, however, we were happily disappointed.

The *Petrel* steamed nearer inshore than had the *Baltimore*, and came to a full stop within a distance of five or six hundred yards of the arsenal.

Then a boat was lowered, and we two lads, together with all the Filipinos, watched eagerly to learn the meaning of this manoeuvre.

Our curiosity was not gratified for some time. After perhaps half an hour had been spent on shore, the

small boat pulled off to the *Petrel* again, and matters
appeared to be in the same condition as before her ar-
rival.

Surely it was perplexing, and the natives exhibited
quite as much disappointment as did my brother and I.

Now came a long time of waiting, or, at least, so it
seemed to us, although no more than three hours elapsed
before the word was passed from one to the other of the
Filipinos that the Spanish troops were marching out of
the fortifications.

Cavité was being evacuated, and our time of deliverance
seemed near at hand.

" We are all right now," Ray said, joyously, throwing his
arms about my neck as if only by some display of affection could he show his great relief of mind.   " We're all
right now, for as soon as these Spaniards have quitted the
town we can make ourselves known to the commander of
the war-vessel, and he must take us on board.   Fancy the
sensation of being among our own countrymen, rather
than this rabble, any one of whom appears ready to
commit murder ! "

The Filipinos moved yet nearer the city, and we followed eagerly, for it was our purpose to show ourselves in
the front as soon as it might be safe, in order to attract
the attention of the Americans.

We were come into what appeared to me to be a
market-place, when the party halted, and from where we
stood — a motley gathering of men, women, and children,
for by this time our numbers were added to by the inhabi-

tants — a good view could be had of the retreating Spaniards, who were marching out fully armed.

Here and there was a native venturesome enough to raise his voice in cries of triumph; but those nearest quickly checked such an outburst, which was in the highest degree dangerous, for men in such mood as were these vanquished soldiers would not hesitate to send a volley among a throng like ours as a means of relieving their own feelings.

Less than half an hour after we were arrived, the last of the troops disappeared in the distance, marching in the direction of Manila, and there was no longer anything to restrain the Filipinos, who, with loud shouts of triumph and menacing cries, rushed forward into the city.

Ray and I went with them because we could do no less while in the midst of such a gathering, and would have done so even had it been possible to choose our own course, for we were advancing toward that point where I believed the Americans were most likely to come ashore.

It had been an hour or more since we last saw Panda; but I had little care as to his absence, because now we needed no guide.

Once we had made ourselves known to the boys in blue, all troubles would be at an end.

While we were crossing the market-place the Filipinos contented themselves with uttering joyous or menacing cries; but once the leaders of the throng were in the vicinity of stores and dwellings their evil instincts burst forth.

In an instant what had been a crowd of people happy in the belief that the cause of freedom was triumphant became a howling, shrieking mob, ready for mischief of any kind, and seeking some living thing on which to wreak revenge for the wrongs endured so long in silence.

It seemed almost incredible that all those men could have changed in appearance, as well as intent, so suddenly. At one moment I saw about me only friendly faces, and in a twinkling Ray and I were surrounded by brutes in human form who panted for blood.

We stood appalled, not knowing which way to turn, when shrieks of pain from a dwelling near by caused us to leap forward, believing it possible to relieve a fellow creature in distress.

There was no question as to the distress; but it was beyond our power to lend a helping hand.

The Filipinos had come upon an old Spaniard, one who, perhaps, had insulted or wronged some of them, and were dragging him from his dwelling that all might participate in the revenge.

The Indians of America could not have been more cruel, or looked upon human agony with greater zest. Even the women tried to force their way among the crowd which surrounded the prisoner, and, failing, threw whatever came nearest at hand at the old man, who was being dragged by the heels back to the market-place.

Ray and I, knowing full well that we could give no aid to the poor wretch, would have gone in the opposite direction, hoping to escape a view of what we knew only too well must follow; but so dense was the throng that we were forced along with that yelling mob despite our frantic efforts to the contrary.

We saw all that followed, for while so many were brandishing weapons it seemed in the highest degree dangerous to close one's eyes even for an instant, and neither of us will ever be able to forget it.

To describe how that old man was tortured would be too horrible even for words, and I rejoiced when death finally came to his relief.

The people were massed so closely around us that we could not move half a dozen inches in either direction until after the terrible spectacle had come to an end, when loud shouts in the distance told that another victim had been found.

The bloodthirsty brutes ran eagerly in the direction indicated by the cries of joy and triumph, and on the instant Ray and I set our faces toward the hills, for we would not advance on a course where we might witness another scene of horror, even in order to meet those who would rescue us from these so-called patriots.

" I had rather skulk around the country a week, or take the chances of making our way back to Manila, than stay here a single minute," Ray said, with a convulsive tremor, which told how deeply the cruel death of the old man had affected him, and I was ready to go wheresoever he proposed, providing the course led us away from these wretched Filipinos.

Hand in hand we ran, believing there would be no

difficulty in finding the warehouse in which we had spent
the night, and from there we could readily gain the open
country.

The streets were thronged with people, some, like ourselves, frightened ; others triumphantly noisy, and yet
more breathing threats of vengeance against those of
Spanish blood.

If our squadron accomplished no more than the freeing
of such as these, then to my mind it was worse than
a waste of ammunition.

The multitude that continued to flow into the city may
have confused us, or, in our agitation, we forgot the direction, turning to the right when we should have gone to the
left ; but whatever the cause we failed to find the
way out of the city, and instead of arriving at the warehouse, we found ourselves in an open square, where a
hundred or more half-naked men were sacking stores and
houses.

These people differed in appearance from Panda's
friends, and I fancied they had come from the interior
of the island, attracted by the reports of the heavy guns ;
but there was no thought either in my mind or Ray's that
we were in any danger from them.

During two or three minutes we stood at one side of
the square trying to determine in which direction we
should proceed, and then I observed four evil-looking
fellows eyeing us in anything rather than an agreeable
manner.

"Look over there!" I whispered. "Those men are

talking about us, and it may not be well to loiter here."

"Surely none of the Filipinos would harm an American after what our vessels did yesterday," Ray replied, with a nervous laugh.

"That may be true; but yet I had rather not have too close an acquaintance with such vicious-looking fellows. A moment ago I hoped we should never see that wretched Panda again; but now I would feel more safe if he were here."

"There is no reason why we should stay, if you are afraid," Ray replied, seizing me by the hand as one would a child, and turning to retrace his steps.

I followed meekly, expecting to feel the blade of a knife in my back at any instant, and wholly unnerved.

Before we had taken a dozen steps the sound of hurried footsteps from the rear told, as plainly as if I had seen all the movements, that we were being pursued.

Now I was the one to lead the way, and at full speed I ran, literally dragging Ray after me, until a hand roughly grasped my shoulder, pulling me backward so violently that I was thrown from my feet.

A cry of anger rather than fear burst from Ray's lips, but I was literally unable to make the slightest sound.

That horrible deed we had witnessed near the market-place was before my eyes, and I believed we were doomed to suffer as had the old man.

Ray, who had managed to retain his footing when the fellows seized us, turned with a brave show of courage, as if ready to meet them empty-handed, facing the gleaming knives without a tremor.

Even though believing absolutely that we would be killed without a show of mercy on the part of any in all that throng, I overcame the stupefaction of terror sufficiently to cry:

"Be careful, Ray, dear! Do not enrage them yet further!"

"Get on your feet and stand by my side!" he cried, sharply. "I'm not minded to hold my head down that these villains may cut my throat the more easily. Stand by me, and we will back them down."

"What can we do against a thousand?" I moaned, in despair.

"Die fighting, if no more!" and the dear boy struck out with his right fist, tumbling one of the half-naked brutes over with a blow full on the neck.

It was the younger who had taken the part of leader, and from that moment until we were finally escaped from danger, I obeyed on the instant any and every order he gave.

His display of bravery had given me some slight show of courage, although the despair in my heart was not lessened, and, regardless of the flourish of knives, I managed to regain my feet, standing close by Ray.

"Get behind me!" he cried. "It must be back to back now, for these brutes would sooner strike a foul blow than a fair one."

"If we can gain time Panda may come up," I whimpered, for I am free to confess that at this trying moment I was a rank coward.

"There's little hope of that, and even if he should let us see his brown face here, I'm uncertain whether it wouldn't be as an enemy. After what our sailors did yesterday, an American should be ashamed to show the white feather, however great the danger, so hold your ground to the last minute."

I was not so terrified but that I could note a certain change of expression on the face of the man directly in front of me when Ray spoke the word "American," and instantly the thought came that it might be possible to make known who we were. Then I cried, at the full strength of my lungs, repeating the words again and again:

"We are Americans! Americans!"

Ray meanwhile was warding off an attack, apparently giving little heed to my shouts.

The foremost of the pursuing party was evidently bent on making us yet closer prisoners, in order, most likely, that we might be the more readily tortured, and had dropped his long knife for the time being.

At such a game my brother could hold his own with any ordinary Filipino, and right manfully was he doing it, dealing a blow now and then with such vigour that the villain was rapidly getting the worst of the battle. Strange as it may seem, his discomfiture pleased those who had gathered to have a share in our death.

Every one of them stood by watching the battle, and my cries were no longer heeded.

" Look out for yourself ! " Ray shouted, when I had half turned to aid him, if necessary. " You should be able to do something of this kind if any of them come too near ! "

To my mind this was but prolonging the agony, and by thus struggling we were affording amusement for the savages, who at any moment might put an end to our

weak defence by attacking us with their knives, when a single thrust would disable one or both.

Therefore it was I continued to cry out that we were Americans, regardless of whether they heeded me, and as I did so there came the hope that the sailors from the war-vessel might soon come this way.

Surely a landing would be effected once it was understood that the Spanish forces had evacuated the place, and even at this moment they might be on shore.

This much I said to Ray, hoping to cheer him who had vainly been trying to cheer me, and he replied, panting with the severe exertion of keeping the supple Filipino at a proper distance :

" I can't hold out much longer, Ernest, and it isn't

likely this murderer will be willing to play at such a game a great while. Once his temper gets the best of him we are done for!"

If Ray was growing disheartened, surely the end was near at hand, for I could not hope to make so brave a showing, and once more I gave way to cowardice.

I thought of mother and of father, wondering if they would ever learn how we had died, and as the tears came into my eyes there was a prayer in my heart that we might not live as long under the torture as had the old man whose murder we had witnessed.

CHAPTER V.

A S we stood there, Ray battling manfully but nearly breathless because of the severe exertions, and I in the last stages of despair, believing there was no hope our lives might be spared, the thought came to me that if by a sudden dash we could make our way to the waterside it would be possible to attract the attention of those on board the American war-vessel.

For a single instant this idea revived me, and then, looking around upon that mass of brown faces which surrounded us, for the crowd of spectators had rapidly increased, I realised that fifty men would not be able to force a passage through, therefore what could two lads hope to effect?

It was when the last vestige of hope was swept away that almost unconsciously I raised my voice once more in the cry:

"We are Americans! Americans!"

Amid the hum of voices and the laughter of those who were enjoying this badgering of two boys before murdering them, I caught a cry in the distance which had a friendly ring, and in the stupefaction of despair which was creeping over me I wondered why it should be, when all were seeking our blood, that any would answer in such a tone what I believed to be my last declaration.

Again was the cry repeated, and Ray, who, because of his courage, was more keenly on the alert, shouted, as he struck his antagonist a blow that would have sent him headlong but for the throng in the rear :

"That was Panda who cried ! There may be a chance for life yet, Ernest ! Take my place until I can get breath ! "

His words had a marvellous effect. In an instant the cowardice and despair had left me, and I thought no longer that we were doomed ; but only of how I might best get the advantage of that half-naked Filipino who was striving to show his followers that he did not deem a weapon necessary in order to overpower two lads like us.

Ray and I changed places in a twinkling, some of the throng giving vent to cries of anger as if they saw in such a move something savouring of foul play ; others cheered, jabbering in such manner as caused me to believe they were insisting that, while the odds were so strongly against us, we should be allowed to carry on the battle in whatsoever manner we pleased.

For a moment the fellow who had pitted himself so unsuccessfully against Ray stood hesitating, breathing heavily as if nearly winded, and for an instant I fancied he was about to retire from the contest, or, perhaps, end it quickly with the long knife which was held conveniently at hand by one of the bystanders.

Then those in the rear urged him on, as I judged from the tone of the voices, and as he advanced, more warily this time, understanding that the lad before him was fresh for the fray, Ray took up the cry which I had been repeating again and again, and immediately was it answered.

There could be no question now but that Panda was coming with all speed to our relief, for his voice sounded nearer than before ; but I had no opportunity to speculate upon the matter, because the Filipino rushed toward me savagely.

At boxing Ray is my superior, although younger, but I knew enough regarding self-defence to hold my own against a man who had most likely never fought save with weapons in his hands, and I could do little more.

The fellow counted on putting an end to the battle quickly by rushing in and seizing me, therefore was I forced to exert all my strength and knowledge.

How long we thus fought at close quarters I know not ; it seemed to me that ten minutes must have elapsed, although probably not more than one-third of that time was spent in warding off his savage rushes, and then, to my intense relief, Panda, with a following of not less than twenty, forced his way through the throng, making such a diversion as caused the brute who counted on taking our lives to fall back momentarily.

There was no longer any idea in my mind that Panda was insolent, or disposed to take advantage of our helplessness, for never before had I seen a face so friendly — certainly never one that was more welcome.

Ray and I received no immediate benefit from the coming of this relief party, however, for during five minutes it appeared as if we were in even greater danger than while alone.

Those who had surrounded us were not inclined to give way, evidently holding to it that our lives belonged to them, and weapons were flourished in such reckless fashion that it seemed as if blood would be spilled unwittingly, because the people were pressed so closely together.

It was Panda's brother who acted as spokesman, and Ray and I fancied he was telling these fiendish Filipinos from the interior that we were Americans, and, consequently, friends; but his appeals, if indeed such they were, failed of success.

First one party would surge toward us, and then the other, until finally, through skilful manœuvring, we were surrounded by Panda's following, and then our would-be protectors grew more bold, massing themselves in a circle, and by their gestures inviting an attack.

"Can't you make them understand who we are?" I asked of Panda, as he turned his head for an instant to look at us.

"My brother has told them again and again; but these people are not Manilamen. They are half Malay, half Chinamen, and see in every white face an enemy."

"Haven't the Americans landed yet?"

"No; they still remain on board their vessel, and the city is being looted by the patriots. Cavité will be destroyed unless your people come on shore soon."

There was no time for further conversation. Panda's brother had given the word to advance, and these brave fellows, who were ready to protect us at the cost of their lives, advanced step by step, still presenting to the enemy a complete circle of steel, with Ray and myself in the centre.

We moved forward no more than twelve inches every minute; but yet it was progress, and once the Malays were giving way it might be possible that we could continue on until a place of safety was gained.

But where should we find such a place until after our troops had landed?

I hoped we were moving toward the water's edge, opposite where the *Petrel* lay; yet I knew she was so far toward the arsenal that a journey of such length, at the snail's pace we were moving, would occupy many hours.

The street in advance and behind us appeared literally choked with human beings; but fortunately not all were bent on our murder. Hundreds upon hundreds were occupied with sacking the stores and the dwellings, and, while giving no heed to such a trifling matter as the slaughter of two lads, they unwittingly impeded our progress by throwing household furniture and goods into the street.

Before ten minutes had passed we were halted, absolutely unable to go farther because the throng in advance was so dense it could not be forced back, and now it was that I saw an expression of apprehension upon the faces of those who guarded us.

Panda's brother spoke sharply and hurriedly to his men, and Ray said to me :

" We are coming to the end of this business very soon. These fellows cannot hope to fight long against so many, and the knowledge that others are getting much plunder only serves to make our enemies the more eager to bring the matter to a finish."

" We will make a stand in this house," Panda said, turning his head ever so slightly toward us. " Be ready to rush in as soon as we gain the door."

He motioned toward a small stone building, on the threshold of which could be seen broken furniture and articles of wearing apparel, showing that it had been gutted by the mob, and although not such a place as one would select for a fort, it looked wonderfully inviting to us at the moment.

Our people, meaning those who were protecting Ray and me, massed themselves yet more closely together for a rush, and then at a signal struck out in every direction.

I saw half a dozen evil-looking faces smeared with blood ; we heard cries of rage which told that the battle would come to a speedy end unless the odds could be made more nearly equal, and then came the rush, during which Ray and I were literally shoved into the dwelling.

For the moment we were safe again, — safe if we could hold our position here until the Americans took possession of the city, which I doubted not they would before many hours elapsed.

In a twinkling the doors were closed, shutters fastened,

and guards stationed at every point where an attempt at forcing an entrance might be made.

Now we had a breathing spell, and it was needed, for Panda's followers had been indulging in most severe exercise.

The Filipino lad took no heed to his own comfort until after making certain we were uninjured, and even then seemed to consider it necessary to assure us again and again that he was sorely grieved because we had been so badly treated.

" Why did you leave us ? " Ray asked, speaking more sharply than I believed to be necessary.

" To see the American vessels. We, all of us Manila-men, believed the soldiers would come on shore at once, and it was not in our minds that these miserable half-breeds would attempt to destroy the city. Wait till General Aguinaldo comes, and you shall see them flogged."

" He, like our own people, seems to be a long while in making his appearance. Cavité is likely to be laid in ashes before the Americans take possession."

" It may be that the commander of the vessel has sent to the fleet for orders," Panda suggested ; but this did not seem to me probable, for, on knowing that the natives were sacking the city, he would first set ashore troops to pro-tect it, and afterward learn what his superior officer thought about the matter.

" How far from here is the American ship?" Ray asked.

" More than four miles."

I was astounded by this information, for Ray and I had believed her to be close at hand. It no longer seemed strange that a delay was made in the landing ; those on board could not know how desperate was the situation on shore.

Ray looked at his watch, believing it to be nearly nightfall, and again we were surprised. It lacked a quarter of an hour of being ten o'clock in the forenoon.

Only five hours since we began to approach the city ! It was to me as if a full day had passed from the moment when the first victim of this mad, purposeless rush was killed.

I looked around the apartment in which we two lads had taken refuge, leaving to the Filipinos the outer rooms where they might keep watch over the mob, and here could be seen evidences of that blind, unreasonable spirit of destruction.

The furniture had been hacked and hewed with swords until not one article remained whole ; rugs were slit into ribbons, and even the hard wooden floor was dented and scratched in such manner as told that one insane with passion had spent both time and labour upon a task which could have no results. It was a scene of wanton destruction such as I do not believe could have been found anywhere outside these islands, and well calculated to alarm those in a position similar to that which we were in, for it showed that murder would be done simply for the sake of killing.

Outside the mob yelled and raved, frenzied because we two lads had for the moment escaped them, and at frequent intervals showers of missiles were sent against the doors and windows, telling that those who thirsted for blood were on the alert.

"Can Panda's friends hold this place?" Ray asked, with a certain tremor in his voice which told that even his courage was giving way under the strain.

The same question had been in my mind from the first moment we sought refuge here, and now as the lad spoke I remembered having seen, before the old man was put to death, certain men tear out blocks of stone from such buildings as showed signs of decay. This was done simply in the spirit of destruction; but it was to me good proof of what might be accomplished in case the howling Malays persisted in their desire to kill us.

"It cannot be long now before troops are put ashore from our vessel," I replied, giving words to the hope in my mind. "Surely we can hold out here until nightfall, and —"

I stopped speaking very suddenly, for at that instant there came a shock, as if the building had been struck by some heavy object, and Panda ran into the room, his face of that grayish hue which bespeaks terror in one of a coloured skin.

"What is it?" Ray cried, seizing the Filipino by the arm, and unconsciously I echoed the words.

"The miserable Malays are striving to destroy the building. Two stones have been removed by force, and this moment a large portion of the corner wall fell down."

He would have said more, but his brother summoned him, and Ray and I, unable to remain where it was impossible to see what might be done, followed him into that apartment overlooking the street.

While we had remained in safety these Filipinos had been battling for our lives, as could be seen by the blood which flowed from more than one wound.

I wondered how it might be that wounds were received when a wall of stone separated us from the enemy, and would have approached one of the windows in order to look out, but Panda's brother pulled me back.

Surely he saved me from an ugly cut, if not from death, for at that instant a knife, lashed to a long length of bamboo, was thrust through an aperture in the thin shell at the very point where I proposed to look out.

The trampling as of many feet on the floor above, and a cry of mingled anger and pain, caused me to look up at the ceiling as if expecting the enemy might appear from that quarter.

" Our friends are up there trying to make payment for some of the wounds we have received," Panda said, and, seizing me by the arm as I turned to ascend the stairs, he added, " It is not for you to join them ; the windows are open, and the Malays must not see you for whom they are seeking."

" We may as well show ourselves as stay here until the house is torn down," Ray cried. " It is better to do something in our own defence than cower here in idleness."

Another shock, and at one corner of the room appeared an aperture in the outer wall through which a man might have crawled.

If the enemy were allowed to work unmolested we must soon be forced to flee to the chamber above, where death would speedily follow.

Then came a great crash ; cries of pain ; a noise as of scampering from the throng outside, and Panda cried, his eyes all aflame with excitement :

" They have thrown out the bed-posts, and some of the villains have been caught napping ! "

It seemed impossible for me to remain there in ignorance of what was being done, and, shaking off the light grasp which Panda had of my arm, I ran up-stairs, Ray following close at my heels.

Now indeed could we see evidences of battle ; two of the Filipinos lay in one corner of the room disabled ; at least five others were covered with blood, and the floor was strewn with stones, fragments of furniture, and even knives, which had been flung in by the mob.

We had come at that moment when a slight advantage had been gained, and, therefore, could approach the open window with some degree of safety.

So far as could be seen in either direction, the streets were literally packed with howling, yelling natives. The work of sacking the city had been abandoned for the moment in order that the villains might enjoy the sport of unearthing two lads whom they probably believed to be Spaniards.

Little chance for life would Ray and I have now if we were in their midst.

It was terrible to look upon those brown-skinned men, knowing that every one was eager to have a hand in the spilling of our blood.

Panda had followed us, and now he pulled me back when I would have lingered at the window.

The attack was about to be resumed; the Malays were drawing near the building once more, and our Manila-men looked about for something more which would serve as weapons.

The huge bedstead, such as is to be found in nearly every house in Luzon, had been thrown out piecemeal, and we had good reason to believe it was not destroyed in vain.

The room was bare of furniture; but there were many rocks on the floor.

These last our men gathered up, each getting one or more, and, standing near the side of the window in such manner as to shield their own bodies, they fired with wonderful accuracy of aim upon those below.

I saw one of our defenders knock down three Malays with as many stones, each of which could not have weighed less than ten pounds, and yet the mob was not checked.

What was the disabling of three men, when a thousand were pressing forward to the attack ?

" However bravely these Manilamen may fight, there can be but one ending to such a battle," Ray said, despondently. " In less than an hour the building will be in possession of those fiends, and we shall have left this world ! "

Now it was my turn to cheer him, even as he had cheered me when my courage failed.

Flinging my arm around his neck, I forced him to the floor below, saying, as we descended the stairs :

" The American troops will have landed before those fellows can tear this house down. It must soon be known to the commander of the *Petrel* that the city is in the hands of a mob, and he will take speedy steps to save it."

" Perhaps he has no troops, but must send back to Manila for men," Ray replied, despondently, and at this suggestion, which seemed most reasonable, I very nearly lost heart again — should have done so, in fact, but for the necessity of cheering my brother.

There was nothing in the room on the ground-floor to

revive our spirits. The corner of the building had been
torn away yet further, until now it was possible to look
into the street through the aperture, and I could see
more than one of the Malays stooping low in order to
fling a knife after the fashion of a spear.

There was an expression of fear on the face of Panda's
brother, and I knew he had begun to despair of holding
the enemy in check much longer.

The Manilamen no longer sought an opportunity to
strike effective blows, but crouched against the wall,
beyond range of the opening.

They had lost heart, and were nerving themselves for
the death which would come to them because of having
dared shield two white lads from harm.

It seemed, indeed, as if the supreme moment had
arrived, and I threw my arms around Ray's neck once
more, hugging him close in what I believed to be a
last embrace, when suddenly the cries of anger from
without were changed to shouts of fear and surprise.

There was no longer any attempt to pull away the
wall; no more rocks were thrown in through the open
windows above. Instead, the throng took to their heels,
and before one could have counted fifty the streets were
cleared as if by magic.

"They have found a victim that can be come at with
less labour," I said, despondently, and then I pricked up
my ears as a great hope, a great joy and relief came into
my heart, causing the blood to bound through every vein.

From the distance, and yet not so far away but that we

could distinguish the tramp, tramp of many feet, came the beat of a drum, the shrill notes of a fife, and this is the tune we two lads, who had believed ourselves face to face with death, heard in the city of Cavité, as we stood within the half-ruined house gripping each other's hands :

> " Yankee Doodle came to town
> Riding on a pony ;
> He stuck a feather in his hat
> And called it macaroni ! "

Never before had I thought there was anything very beautiful in that song ; but now it seemed the sweetest I ever heard, and since then it amuses me as can no other combination of notes.

Singing at the full strength of our lungs, what was at the same time a song of triumph and of thanksgiving, Ray and I flung open the door, for the Filipinos had begun to unbar it instantly the shrill notes of the fife were heard, marching into the street, with the Manilamen at our heels, to meet our countrymen.

I wish it might be possible for me to set down all that followed after we made ourselves known ; but it cannot be done, and for the good reason that neither Ray nor I have any very clear idea of anything until we found ourselves on the deck of the *Petrel*, explaining to Commander Lamberton how we two Yankee lads chanced to be in Cavité.

Within forty-eight hours we were with our parents again, and there is no need for me to set forth at any very great length our joy at meeting them once more.

As is well known, Manila did not surrender for some time after the city of Cavité was taken possession of by our forces, and if it should chance that this poor story of mine is ever printed, I shall request permission to try my hand at story-writing again, in order to set down the part Ray and I played in the capitulation of the port, for we had no mean adventure in the island of Luzon after the rescue of Cavité, as is known already to very many.

At present it is sufficient to say that we were present when the Spanish forces finally capitulated, and we met Aguinaldo face to face many times more than was really agreeable; but all this occurred after we had our experience among the Filipinos, when Dewey came to Cavité, therefore it is not anything which can properly be set down here.

THE END.